Nelly
and the
Quest for
Captain Peabody

BY ROLAND CHAMBERS

ILLUSTRATED BY ELLA OKSTAD

OXFORD
UNIVERSITY PRESS

CHAPTER ONE

At the end of the pier was a boat that looked like a pile of broken sticks floating on the water. Nobody had sailed in it for years, and all the paint had peeled off.

It had an old-fashioned ship's wheel, of the sort you get on pirate ships and it was dotted with tiny holes where woodworm were eating it. It had two masts, a long one and a short one, and was bound to the pier—or jetty, or quay, or pontoon, or whatever you want to call it—by an ancient rope from which hung green beards of seaweed that smelled of stale oysters.

At one end of the rope was the boat, and at the other sat Nelly, cross-legged with her chin in her hands, while her pet turtle, Columbus, dozed in the sun. Columbus was a very sleepy turtle, but when he woke up he always had a look in his eye as if he'd been somewhere interesting and wasn't going to tell you where it was.

The girl was called Nelly and the boat was called *Nelly*, just the same. It belonged to Captain Bones Peabody, of the Gentlemen's Exploratory Flotilla, who had gone off many years before with a group of gentlemen explorers to sail around the world and, as yet, had not returned. Nelly, the girl, was Captain Peabody's daughter, and she missed her father although she couldn't remember meeting him. All she knew was that his post piled up in a bin in the hall, and that he collected exotic snails. They crawled along the backs of chairs and the tops of picture frames. They were dotted along the banisters of the stairs and hung upside down from

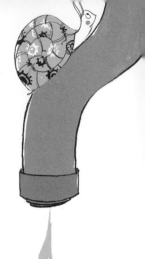

the frames of doors, and sometimes, when Nelly was thirsty in the middle of the night and went for a drink of water, she would find one clinging to the mouth of the tap in the bathroom, which was disgusting. Some of the larger ones had painted shells.

Nelly missed her father, but her mother hardly noticed, either the snails or anything else, because she was always knitting. She knitted scarves, hats, and mittens, hundreds of them, which she packed into boxes and sent off with the postman once a fortnight. It was amazing how many hats, scarves,

and mittens she knitted, and this was why she never minded the snails, or Nelly, or Columbus, or the missing sailor. Nelly's mother was like a sleepwalker; she lived in a world of her own.

On this particular day—the first real day of summer—Nelly sat cross-legged on the pier and talked to Columbus.

'The difficulty,' she explained, 'is that we have no sails . . . '

Which was true, the sails had rotted away years and years ago.

'. . . and without sails,' continued Nelly, looking at the palms of her hands, 'the adventure I have in mind will be impossible. Are you curious to know what it is?'

But Columbus was asleep and didn't answer.

'We're going to find my father,' explained Nelly, 'and on the way we can have some other adventures, with pirates, waterspouts, and so forth. The only difficulty is that we have nothing to catch the wind in, but I have a plan for that, too. I shall knit a set of sails using Mother's knitting needles. They won't be canvas, exactly, but our sails will be softer and warmer than the usual kind, and I shall use the pointiest needles. I shall do it at night, secretly, and you shall stand guard.'

And that is exactly what happened, because if Nelly said she was going to do a thing, she did it, whatever it was. Sometimes she would say, 'I'm going to lie in bed all day,' and at other times, 'I shall learn the recipe for gunpowder.' It was part of her code, and now she'd said she was going to find her father, Captain Bones Peabody of the Gentlemen's Exploratory Flotilla, in a boat with knitted sails, and she meant it.

So Nelly crept downstairs that night and knitted, while Columbus kept watch with one eye open and the other closed, and she did the same the next

night and the next. CLICKETY-CLICK, went the needles, CLICKETY-CLICK, like the sound of teeth chattering, or the tips of bony crabs' legs as they scuttle across rocks, or desperate cutlasses criss-crossing in the distance. And while she knitted, she thought of the voyage ahead, and her father, wherever he might be—in the jungle or on the top of a mountain

or the tip of an iceberg—looking just as
he did in the portrait of him that hung in
the hall, wearing a three-cornered hat, and
holding up a postcard, with an expression
on his face that suggested he couldn't find
a postbox.

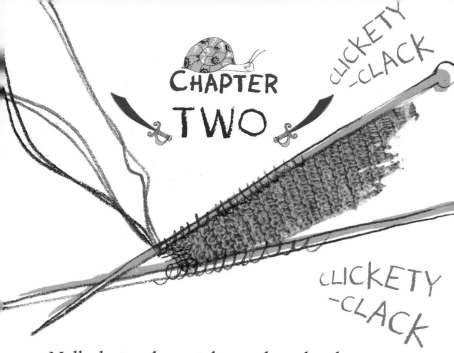

CHAPTER TWO

CLICKETY
-CLACK

CLICKETY
-CLACK

Nelly knitted at night, and in the day saw to everything else. She varnished the decks and painted the hull. She sewed flags to signal with and laid in new ropes, and what she couldn't make herself or find lying about the house she ordered from Messrs Fiennes, Hilary, and Scott Ltd, who supplied gentlemen explorers with everything necessary to launch an expedition. Down in the hold, tightly packed to stop them rolling about in a storm, were barrels of cheese, beans, salt pork, and chocolate biscuits, and also lemons and limes because

Nelly had read that if you don't eat enough vitamins on a long voyage you get scurvy, which makes your teeth fall out. She also ordered maps, a compass, a telescope, a ship's megaphone, an inflatable rubber dingy, and a retired cabin boy to look after her mother while she was away.

Aboard the *Nelly*, which Captain Peabody had named after his daughter (or was it the other way round?), was a small kitchen, a bathroom, and a cabin with a hammock and a library. There were cupboards for clothes and fishing tackle and pots and pans, and beside the barrels of pork and cheese in the hold was a barrel of gunpowder and a coal scuttle full of cannon balls for two small cannons on deck. The cannons were shaped like Chinese dogs, with open mouths and curly tails, and had come from Captain Peabody's study, where they had stood on either side of his fireplace.

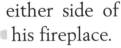

It took Nelly a week to knit the sails, and another to prepare her boat, but as she worked by day and also by night she squeezed two weeks into one. She was used to hard work because she had always done everything for herself. She cooked, and was good at it. She mended her clothes, and did the laundry, and even managed the household accounts because her mother paid no attention to such things and never had. Not that Nelly's mother didn't care for her: at bedtime she told her stories or sang her songs, and in the garden, close by the rhubarb patch, she had planted her an apple tree.

So Nelly managed things her own way, as she always had, and prepared her boat as if it were a house on the water. She ordered two spare mop heads and a whole box of broom handles. She ordered a sack of wool, to repair holes in her sails, and half-a-dozen toothbrushes. She ordered enough clean towels (including tea towels) to last six months, as well as two dozen complete sets of underwear, and a bottle of ammonia

11

because she had read about a clever way to wash your clothes involving dustbin liners. She ordered so many things that the postman used up all the ink in his pen just ticking each item off his list; so it was fortunate that he had another pen, a whole row of them gleaming in his breast pocket. But he never seemed to mind the work. He carried all the boxes himself and never seemed to notice Nelly, although when her mother appeared (with a hot-water bottle or a spool of new wool) he would sigh and wipe his forehead with a red silk handkerchief.

Nelly's boat had compartments for wet gear and dry gear, for clean and also dirty laundry, and in her cabin was a table that hung from the ceiling by ropes so that nothing would spill off it in bad weather. It was for eating at, but also for studying maps and plotting a course, and for consulting her ship's library, which included the *Encyclopaedia of Marine Life*, the *Explorer's Companion*, and a diary bound in black leather she had found in her father's desk. At the front of it was a list of things he had ordered for a voyage of his own, and at the back a list of things he had thought it important to remember after he had set sail:

1. Don't forget N's birthday!
2. Back in a year.
3. Don't go native!

But of course Captain Peabody had forgotten almost all of Nelly's birthdays, and had not come back in anything close to a year, and whether or not he had gone native (whatever that meant) Nelly still had no idea where she might find him, or even where to start looking. She had read his memoir, *Captain Peabody Goes Out*. She knew that he had sailed to the West Indies, and across the South China

Sea, and to the Ivory Coast, where his ship had been mistaken for a pirate ship. She knew that he had sent her a turtle egg in a cake tin for her first birthday, along with a box of snails with painted shells, but she had no idea where the turtle had come from or if Captain Peabody had painted the snails himself. She had never received a letter from him, or a postcard, or even a telegram, and when she asked her mother when he was coming home, Mrs Peabody would just sigh and suggest a game of cards or ask her daughter to help her with the crossword puzzle. Nelly didn't even know if her father was alive or if he was already an extinct explorer, just as the woolly mammoth and the dodo are extinct.

'Where have you all got to?' she whispered, looking up at a photograph of Captain Peabody and his colleagues, the so-called Gentlemen of the Exploratory Flotilla, all bearded men with pipes in their mouths, standing in two rows behind their captain who was holding a medal with an expression on his face that suggested he was wondering what to do with it.

But of course none of them answered, so Nelly got on with the business at hand: preparing her ship by day and knitting all night, with only Columbus to keep her company. Clickety-click went her needles, as she thought how big the world was, how dark and deep the seas, and yet the sails grew under her hands and spread out across her knees and the floor until they began to push out of the sitting room. And on the morning of the eighth day, just as the sun was coming up, she cast off.

CHAPTER
THREE

Nelly's sails were striped with bright colours, like rainbows, and knitted with the sharpest needles. When the wind blew hard it spilled from the tops of them like water splashing out of a spoon, and for the first few days the wind blew so well and so evenly Nelly didn't have to think about where she was going, or what she was doing, at all. So she tied the ship's wheel in place with a carefully knotted handkerchief and slept for a week, dreaming with Columbus as she had done for as long as she could remember, ever since she was a baby.

When Columbus was awake he was not a talkative turtle. What he did best was keep calm and look wise. He didn't play cards or chess, and he wasn't much help around the ship because he couldn't tie knots or reef the sails or swab the decks. But when he was asleep, he dreamed amazing dreams, and sometimes Nelly dreamed them too. She dreamed she was still in her egg and heard seagulls overhead. She dreamed of her father sitting at his desk, and of another room far away, with a rocking chair and a stove and bookshelves lined with jam jars and leaves rustling outside square windows. She dreamed of a white mountain that steamed like a kettle, and a painted stone and a lake of fire around which a crowd of small men danced, bearded and covered in tattoos, naked except for woolly hats, scarves, mittens and socks, and bits of cloth around their waists that looked suspiciously like the tea towels she had ordered from the Fiennes, Hilary, and Scott catalogue.

Sometimes Nelly dreamed Columbus's dreams and sometimes she dreamed her own—that she had left the oven on in her mother's kitchen, or a tap running, or had forgotten to mend the roof. She dreamed of unposted letters and a dozen cardboard boxes in the hall she had forgotten to unpack and worried that the cabin boy might not have found the note she had left in the kitchen, with a list of instructions about household management. Or that her mother might have missed the one in the sitting room in which Nelly said goodbye and promised she would be back in a year.

And then she woke up and realized the sound of running water was the sea splashing against the sides of her boat, and that the swaying was her hammock, rocking her in its arms, and when she went up on deck the sea was blue and unblinking all the way to the horizon, without any shadow of land.

Nelly weighed anchor in springtime, and for a month the weather was fine. In the mornings she would wake and scrub the decks, then make breakfast, then settle down in her favourite chair before the mast, with the brightly knitted sails humming above her, and read a book or snooze, with Columbus for a footstool. Sometimes she would practise tying knots and sometimes magic tricks, and sometimes she would drop a sea anchor and go swimming, with a rope tied round her waist to make sure the *Nelly* didn't drift off without her. She swam on the surface of the water and Columbus swam below, and at night she dreamed of the things he had seen: of angel fish and parrot fish. Of eels striped like zebras, and sunlight disappearing into the deep where prawns shone like stars and the dimly seen bodies of enourmous creatures moved in the watery night.

'Whales,' Nelly wrote in her log one evening, and drew a picture in crayon to show what they had looked like. They had come so close to her in the water that she could almost touch them, and when she climbed back on board they swam around the boat. They peered at Nelly through small, kind eyes, and romped very gently, as

though her ship were a bubble they didn't want to pop; and then, with a snort, they were gone.

And that was how the first few weeks went by. Nelly got up and did her chores. She had breakfast. She read her book and swam. She taught herself to whistle by sticking her fingers in her mouth, and to juggle china cups, which takes a lot of practice. The water was always shining, the wind was never too boisterous, and standing on deck beneath her rainbow sails, with her own flag fluttering above her, Nelly felt as though she were a queen in her own country and the empress of the ocean. In fact, everything went so easily for such a long time that she began to feel that sailors who boast of daring adventures on the high seas must exaggerate just to impress people.

And then one morning, as she was making breakfast, the rigging began to whine and the sky turned black in the time it took to fry an egg.

CHAPTER
FOUR

When Nelly sailed into her first storm it was as though a thousand shouting mouths had opened in the water. Everything was purple, yellow, and black; everything was wet and salty; everything whipped and cracked and roared as it smashed into splinters or swooshed across the deck. Everything got mixed up in everything else—wet things and dry things, safe things and dangerous things—so that at times it was difficult to tell where the sea ended and the boat began, except that the boat was all there was between Nelly and drowning.

So Nelly fought to keep it afloat. She reefed the sails to make them small. She steered into the wind so it did not boss her about. When waves crashed over the deck, and poured into the hold, she scooped the water out with a bucket. But however hard she fought the wind fought harder, and the waves piled up higher so that the sky was all water, lashing down rain and foam and battering her with great fists as if the ocean were alive and really hated her—except that it didn't even know she was there. When the lightning blistered she could see the ropes of her ship like cracks in glass, but she had no time to feel sorry for herself because everything was happening at once: the screech of nails trying to pull out of wood, the ship spinning, teetering for a moment high up on top of a mountain of water before—swoosh!—racing down again into the valleys.

In the middle of the storm there was so little difference between the sea and the air that it was hard to breathe without drowning. Nelly was always gasping and choking, ducking and staggering, then heaving herself up to wrestle with the wheel, or to haul down the sails, because even after making them small the wind was bossing her completely, and

she was getting too tired to boss back. It was better to let the storm have its way and hope it would blow itself out, although there was no sign that it would. On it howled, hour after hour, day after day, until Nelly couldn't remember a time when there had been no storm, and had no energy in any case to think about it. It felt as though she had always been a girl in a yellow oilskin sou'wester, scooping water with a tin bucket, waiting for the wave that would smash her to pieces, until, just as suddenly as it had started, it was over and she went to bed.

This time, when Nelly woke up her pillow was covered in grains of salt and her knees and elbows were bruised from so much bashing about. But there was no serious damage, and Columbus (who had spent the whole time tucked in his shell under Nelly's duvet) was only slightly scuffed around the edges. So after breakfast she gave him a rub with an oily rag, and then went over her ship with a hammer and a screwdriver. She patched her sails and mended her ropes. She made sure of the lids on the barrels in her hold. But just as she was settling down with a cup of tea in her second favourite deck chair (her favourite one had been swept overboard) there was another storm, and after that another, and just as she was getting used to storms she was nearly swallowed up by a whirlpool.

The whirlpool started as a small black **dot** on the water, then widened like the thread of a screw until the *Nelly* was on the edge of a funnel with steep WOBBLING sides that made a **roaring**, *sucking* sound as if the whole ocean were going down the plughole.

If Nelly had gone in, she had no idea where she would have ended up because she couldn't see the bottom. But she didn't go in. The wind caught her sails and, just as she was lifted up and out, the sea closed behind her with a monstrous, gurgling burp.

Nelly wrote down everything in her log, and drew pictures of the most interesting bits with her crayons: the first storm, the whirlpool, a shoal of flying fish, a shark that hit its head against the side of the boat. One evening the rigging lit up suddenly with tiny cold blue flames, which she discovered from her *Explorer's Companion* were called St Elmo's fire. On another somebody tapped her on the shoulder while she was reading her book, and when she turned to see who it was saw two enormous tentacles snaking out of the water. Together they felt all over the ship, like the fingers of a blind person, but when they came to Nelly's washing, hanging from the rigging in dustbin bags, they whipped back as if they'd been burned, which Nelly put down to the ammonia.

'Giant octopus,' she wrote in her log, and drew it with her crayons, beginning with the huge eyes she had seen sinking away from her into the gloom with a reproachful expression, as if the octopus had only wanted to say hello.

Worst of all, though, were the days when nothing happened; when the sails hung limp as old cardigans and there was nothing to do but think. Columbus's birthday was in July, but there were no eggs to bake a cake. On Halloween they had no pumpkin, and the thought of ripe apples lying in the grass at home was enough to make her cry, not just because she was homesick, but because she was hungry, too. By then she had been at sea for months and her stores were getting low. She had some salt pork left, but she had run out of chocolate. Soon she would have to live off cheese, and when she ran out of cheese she would be left with lemons and hard tack biscuits. If she ran out of lemons, she wouldn't have teeth, and without teeth how could she eat the tack?

More frightening still was the thought of the ship coming apart: the planks rotting, the mast breaking in high winds, the ropes snapping, the sails tearing and there being no more wool to mend them. It was bound to happen some time, and there was no end to the voyage in sight because Nelly still didn't know where her father was, or even if, after months and months of searching, she was any closer to him than she had been when she started. Probably she was further away.

'It seems to me,' she told Columbus, 'that looking for a lost sailor on the high seas is a lot like being lost yourself.'

But of course Columbus didn't answer, so Nelly went back to sucking her lemon, because by then she had run out of water, and although it was nearly Christmas the sun was hotter than it had been in August. Not that she felt particularly Christmassy anyway. For weeks she had been plugging leaks between the shrinking planks with tea towels dipped in tar, but now even the tea towels had run out, and the *Nelly*'s sails, which had been so colourful, looked as if they'd been knitted from old ladies' hair.

Only the things outside the ship were bright and strong. The sun was yellow and the sea was a daylight blue that went on and on for miles and miles and miles, without anything to get in the way, without anything to interrupt it, smooth and unblinking . . . except that on this particular day there seemed to be something out there after all.

At first Nelly thought she had a fleck of wool in her eye and rubbed it, but it didn't go away. She went to fetch her telescope, and it was still there, but much nearer. It wasn't land, as she'd hoped, but neither was it a whale. It was like a drop of blood floating on the water.

'Pirates!' she shouted, which woke Columbus up properly.

CHAPTER FIVE

The pirate ship was painted red, every bit of it. The planks were red and the sails were red. Even the ropes were red, as if they had been dipped in the blood of past victims. In fact, the only bit of the ship that wasn't painted red was the flag fluttering from the top of its highest mast, which Nelly recognized from her book of signal flags. It was black, with a white skull and crossbones.

'Perhaps they haven't seen us,' she whispered, although the pirates were coming straight for them. 'Or perhaps we can make friends.' But that didn't seem very likely either.

Nelly had read about the horrible things that pirates do—the terrible tortures— and wondered what it would feel like to be scraped to pieces by barnacles or eaten alive by crabs or flogged with a cat o' nine tails. She wondered if it only hurt at the beginning or all the way through, and if dying was like falling into a hole or going to sleep or lying in a box and having somebody close the lid on top of you. And then she saw a second flag go up the mast to join the skull and crossbones. It was red.

'No prisoners!' she gasped. 'Which means they'll kill us even if we *do* surrender. Not that it makes much difference. We'd have died of thirst anyway.'

Nelly's ship was quick, but the pirate ship was quicker and far bigger. Through the eye of her telescope it looked like a city on the water, with hundreds of sails crowded one on top of the other, each sail dyed blood red and filled with a hot, irresistible wind. It grew larger and more terrifying as it came closer, until Nelly could make out its figurehead: a roaring dragon with its mouth open and its tongue sticking out.

'Oh Columbus!' cried Nelly when she saw it, and thought how unfair it was that she was so young and had nobody at all to help her; that her parents had not cared for her better; that she had been forced to do all the cleaning as well as the household accounts when other children were playing in the bath with rubber ducks. She thought of all the brave men in uniform posing for portraits in the hall at home, beautifully framed, carrying swords or muskets or flags, and how every one of them, including her father, had abandoned her, and tears poured down her cheeks, right there in the middle of the ocean, which is made entirely of salt water. They fell in great wobbly drops and made dark spots on the deck—those, at least, that did not land on the back of Columbus's head.

And then Nelly laughed and cracked her knuckles with a horrible unladylike popping sound.

'The dogs!' she growled. 'They'll be sorry

they ever laid eyes
on me.'
   And she hoisted
her own flag: a green
turtle stitched onto
black cloth,

followed by a red
handkerchief to
signal that she
didn't intend to
take prisoners
either.
   And, of course,
when Nelly said a
thing, she meant it.

CHAPTER SIX

Far off on the horizon the pirate ship had looked like a fleck of red wool or a drop of blood, but soon, peering through her telescope, Nelly could see dark figures climbing in the rigging, and a name, *The Penny Red* picked out in gold at its prow. Men crawled everywhere about it, up and down, straining, hauling. She could see the immense size of it, the many squares of canvas, the dragon figurehead, the Jolly Roger, and the red flag that meant no quarter. But at first she could not hear it. The pirate ship was like a phantom, like death itself swooping down on her, until she could see the rusty heads of the nails that pinned its planks and the stitching on its sails and the puffs of smoke springing from dark holes in its sides.

And then, suddenly, there *was* noise: the blast of exploding gunpowder.

Nelly wasn't ignorant or defenceless. She had read about battles at sea in a book. She knew what a broadside was, and a fighting top. She knew what grappling irons were, and about waiting until you could see the whites of your enemy's eyes. Down in her kitchen was a whole collection of kitchen knives, as well as a box of matches. In her knitting basket were the pointiest knitting needles, and up on deck were the Chinese dogs she had taken from her father's study, along with barrels of gunpowder and the coal scuttle full of cannonballs. Nelly had everything she needed to fight a battle, except having actually fought a battle. She had never been attacked by pirates, or even seen a pirate—not a real one—but of course there is a first time for everything.

'Man the cannons!' Nelly shouted, while Columbus danced forward and backward with his neck stretched out and his mouth open. He was very anxious and frightened, and a little confused, too, but Nelly wasn't. She felt it all at once, so that the pirate ship and the match in her hand, the fizz of the Chinese dogs' curly tails (which were fuses) and the jolt of the explosions, were all one thing. And when she saw the smoke of her guns she felt like singing.

'ROOOAAAARRRR!!!!' went the pirate ship, and Nelly's dogs barked back, first one, then the other, sending up showers of splinters from the red ship as they hit their mark. But all the same her guns were so much smaller than the guns of *The Penny Red*, and there were far fewer of them: just two small dogs against a whole army of cannons, a great red cliff of cannons all firing at once.

'ROOOOAAAARRR!!!!'
'ROOOOAAAARRR!!!!'

went the pirate ship, and the air was filled with the whizz and hiss of red-hot iron. One ball tore through the *Nelly*'s rigging, another brought down her tallest mast, and through the smoke and thunder came the dragon with its mouth open and a figure standing on the very tip of its tongue: the pirate captain himself, holding a rope in one hand and a cutlass in the other, dressed all in red and grinning a horrible grin.

The pirate captain had a red silk handkerchief tied around his head and ruby earrings. His red shirt was sewn with red buttons and his boots were made of red leather. The hand that held his cutlass was clenched in a red glove, and the inside of his mouth was red, too, though his teeth were small and white.

'Invincible!' he screamed, swinging down onto Nelly's deck, and if she hadn't ducked just in time her journey would have ended.

Up and down they fought, jumping on

INVINCIBLE!!!

the gunwales, swinging from the rigging,
stepping sideways like crabs; but all the
while, as Nelly parried with her kitchen
knife (the one she used for slicing
cabbages) and lunged with her knitting
needle, she couldn't help thinking that

the pirate looked familiar. It wasn't his ruby earrings or his red velvet waistcoat. It wasn't the thin-lipped smile, or the gold buckles of his boots, and it certainly wasn't his red satin knickerbockers buttoned at the knee.

Perhaps he's a friend of my mother's, she wondered, but she knew perfectly well her mother didn't have any friends, and besides, she couldn't remember meeting anybody quite so fond of one colour.

Or maybe I've seen his photograph in the Fiennes, Hilary, and Scott catalogue?

It was a highly unusual and preposterous situation; perplexing, infuriating and distracting, but the thing was that when Nelly rummaged around for the sort of person he might be she didn't find herself looking in the pirate drawer at all, or even the ruffian drawer, but a different drawer altogether: something to do with headed notepaper and sharpened pencils.

And while she was racking her brains, the fight went on.

SWOOSH

went the pirate's cutlass.

SWASH

So that at any moment the question might not matter, because there would be nobody around to ask it. A portrait in the lavatory? A dream? A simple case of déjà vu? Nelly fished around for the answer and at the same time she fought for her life, skipping and parrying, ducking and cartwheeling, until, with a clever twist of his wrist and a howl of delight, the pirate winkled the kitchen knife out of her hand and sent it spinning into the water.

UNSTOPPABLE! he screeched, giving Nelly a close up of his sharp white teeth and tonsils. But as he stepped forward with his cutlass raised there was a flash between Nelly's ears like a silent cannon going off.

'Of course,' she said. 'You're the postman!'

'I am not!' said the pirate captain.

'Oh yes you are,' said Nelly. 'Look, I can see your pens.'

And there they were, gleaming in a row in his top pocket, just as she'd seen them at home.

CHAPTER

SEVEN

When Nelly woke up she was lying in a hammock, but it wasn't her hammock, in a cabin that wasn't her cabin. There was a desk in the corner with a red leather top, and red curtains on the windows, which had many tiny panes of glass. The wallpaper was red and the carpet was red, and from a hook on the door hung the postman's red pirate uniform and cutlass. Everything was red except the sea and the man sitting beside her, who had changed his red velvet waistcoat and knickerbockers for a white shirt and freshly pressed black trousers. In his hand he held a glass of water, and the expression on his face was tender.

'How are you feeling?' he asked.

'How are you feeling?' said Nelly, who remembered how he'd looked as he prepared to cut her down the middle. But she wasn't frightened anymore. The water was refreshing, the hammock comfortable, and when she wriggled her toes she could feel Columbus lying at the other end of it.

'Much more myself,' confessed the postman-pirate.

'Whatever that means,' laughed Nelly. 'First you're a pirate, and then you're a postman, which is the opposite. Or were you a pirate all along?'

'I couldn't say,' admitted her host, polishing a pair of gold-rimmed spectacles. 'When I'm a postman I'm a postman, and when I'm a pirate I'm a pirate. You may tell me, for example, that this morning I attacked your ship and tried to murder you in cold blood.'

'And so you did, don't try to deny it!'

'But I can't remember a thing about it,' he shrugged. 'Perhaps it's the weather, or maybe the work. It's not easy, you know, especially at Christmas—so many presents, so many cards; racing all over the place to get them delivered in time. And the paperwork!'

He sighed and showed Nelly his hands, though as far as she could tell there was nothing particularly special about them; a little inky perhaps. 'Sometimes, I suppose,

I erupt into piracy.'

'I should report you to the Post Office,' said Nelly.

'Certainly you should.'

'But I have a better idea. You see, I happen to be looking for somebody, but I don't know where he is, and since you're the postman you're bound to have his address. In fact I know you do because you deliver all his letters. You come once every fortnight, and you take them away, along with my mother's knitting.'

'And who is this person?' asked the postman.

'My father,' replied Nelly. 'Captain Peabody of the Gentlemen's Exploratory Flotilla.'

The name had such an electrifying effect on the postman that for a moment Nelly was worried he might be about to turn back into a pirate again. His nostrils, which had black hair sprouting from them, widened, and his eyes turned icy blue. His lips drew back from his teeth, and even his moustache seemed blacker and more pointy than before. Nelly marvelled that a face could hold two such different people in it.

'Do you know him?' she asked.

'Know him?' said the postman, grinding his teeth but remaining, Nelly was relieved to note, seated. 'Of course I know him. Bones Peabody who discovered the salt-water caterpillar. Bones Peabody who won the Admiral's Cup for Night-Time Navigation six years in a row. Old Bones who graduated top of his class and played first violin in the academy orchestra. Know him, of course I know him! Captain Bones Peabody who married the most beautiful girl in the navy,' he groaned. 'And you say you're his daughter?'

'I am,' said Nelly.

'Well, I might have guessed it,' said the postman, sadly looking at Nelly's hair. 'But all the same I can't tell you where he is.'

'Yes you can! You're the postman; you deliver the post. You know where everybody lives.'

'Maybe I do and maybe I don't, but all the same, rules are rules.'

'What rules?'

'Post Office rules,' and for a moment he

looked so smug she wanted to slap him. 'I don't make them and I can't break them. It's more than my job's worth.'

'Oh you fool!' shouted Nelly, and burst into tears. She wished they were toe to toe again on the deck of the *Nelly* so she could murder him properly. She wished she could scrape him to death with barnacles or flog him with a cat o' nine tails, and as she wished it she cried, because she was angry and hungry, and because she had come such a long way and was no better off than when she had started. She wept and imagined the terrible things she would like to do to him: death by drowning, death by burning, death by flaying alive, and as she wept the postman begged her to stop. He wrung his hands, he offered her his scarlet handkerchief, he took off his spectacles and put them on again, and stared at the ceiling making faces—and then (because he understood the depth of her frustration) he gave in.

'Oh very well,' he said, 'if it means that much to you.'

CHAPTER
EIGHT

Nelly and Columbus ate Christmas dinner with the crew of *The Penny Red*, who didn't seem at all alarmed by their captain's changeable character. They had on grey uniforms and ate Christmas pudding with the same expressions they wore when they did the washing up, which was no expression at all. But what they lacked in personality they made up for in hard work. They scrubbed the *Nelly*'s decks and replaced her broken mast with a spar from their own ship, which fitted

perfectly. They filled the empty barrels in her hold. They polished her brass and freshened her paint, and while they were at it Nelly mended the holes in her sails with bright new wool.

Everything was done that is possible to do for a boat that is still at sea, and when Nelly and Columbus were ready to go the postman saw them off, looking, she thought, rather lonely as he waved goodbye.

Nelly sailed on New Year's Day, and at first the wind blew strong and evenly. By her side was a cutlass with a red handle that the postman had given her as a Christmas present, and on her vest a dragon brooch with flashing ruby eyes. In her hold were letters and parcels and wooden crates full of knitting to be delivered to Captain Peabody and his crew, along with a gold watch for her father and a box of red silk handkerchiefs for her mother. But best of all was a chart with a cross on it showing the position of her father's ship, which was close to the top of the world and a little to the right.

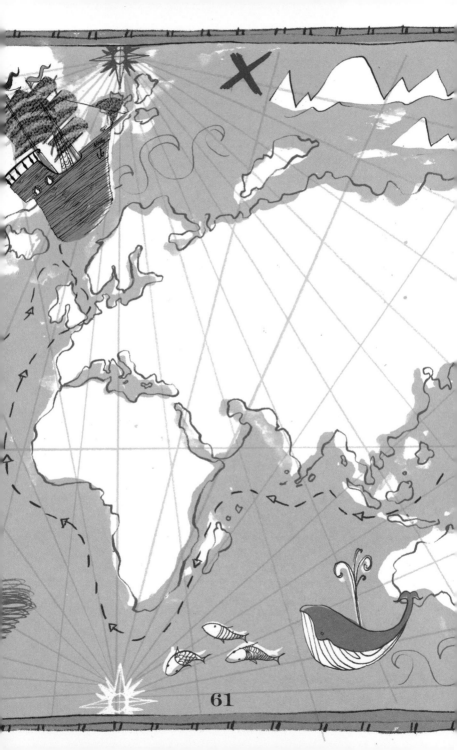

Everything seemed set fair, and Nelly sang for joy, because she sailed on Post Office business and knew secrets only the Post Office knew. Around her bows, dolphins played, looking, she thought, as much like whales as kittens do cats. They had pale bellies and sharp little teeth, and as they turned to study Nelly with one eye, then the other, they seemed to smile. But one morning, much to her surprise, the water in the kitchen sink went down the plughole in the wrong direction, and soon it was chilly enough for her to need stockings on deck. There were sudden squalls and flurries of rain, and a couple of weeks after the dolphins disappeared she saw her first waterspout.

Whereas whirlpools suck you down, waterspouts suck you up, but they are just as terrifying, if not more so. They are a whirlwind at sea and this one came down from the clouds like an enormous elephant's trunk searching in the water. It hissed and writhed this way and that, so that Nelly couldn't tell if it was heading straight for her or would pass her by, and the closer it came the more clearly she could see what was inside it: seaweed, small squid, an entire shoal of sardines swirling round and round as sardines do when they are under-water, except these ones were swirling up a transparent tube, along with sharks, an octopus and yellowfin tuna.

It came so close that Nelly was sure she would be sucked up, too, and forced to live in a cloud until the next time it rained; but just as she could feel the spray of it on her face it broke apart with a fizz, and onto the deck fell a shower of silver fish the size of her finger.

Nelly fried up the fish with a squeeze of lemon and drew an arrow in her log to show that the waterspout had been spinning in a clockwise direction. The next morning she pulled on a pair of woolly tights and mittens, and in the evening drank a cup of cocoa, which was possible because the postman—who was amazed she had done without it for so long—had given her a barrel of cocoa powder.

'And is my father a pirate, too?' she had asked him.

'Probably not' he replied, 'but he is a collector, which is just as bad, if not worse.'

'And did you really know him as a boy?'

'Certainly! We grew up almost as brothers.'

'But not actually brothers?'

'Not actually brothers, no. We didn't have any family at all.'

'Orphans then?' asked Nelly hopefully.

'Orphans,' confirmed the postman.

Which made Nelly want to ask more questions, but seeing how the postman's nostrils flared she decided against it.

'Now dress up warm,' he told her, 'and don't forget to give your mother the handkerchiefs.'

CHAPTER

NINE

Nelly had left home in springtime, when her apple tree was blossoming and the sun was bright and hot. She had sailed south and the sun had followed her, getting hotter all the time, until she reached almost to the bottom of the world, where it is Christmas Day in the middle of summer. But now she was sailing due north, where it is cold all year round, and the closer she came to the cross on the postman's map, the less she knew what to expect when she got there. She had never met her father, or even received a letter from him. She didn't know what his voice sounded like, or if he was tall or short. In fact, until she had met the postman the only reason she had known he was alive at all was that her mother sometimes talked about him as if he had only that moment stepped out of the room.

'Your father likes rhubarb crumble,' she would say in the middle of lunch. Or over tea: 'When Captain Peabody gets in, I think I'll bake a Victoria sponge.'

But Captain Peabody did not get in, and while Nelly was waiting for him she had built him out of the things he had left behind: the books on his bookcase and the souvenirs on his mantelpiece, the blotting paper on his desk and the bronze dogs on either side of his fireplace. She had read his memoirs and stood in the hallway and stared at his portrait, along with the portraits of her relatives and the Gentlemen of the Exploratory Flotilla. But she didn't know who he was any more than she knew what was in the letters and parcels in her hold (apart, that is, from her mother's knitting), and when she tried to imagine him it was like looking down a well, or at the blank face of the moon, which grew larger as she sailed north, like a peephole onto a brilliantly lit room.

Soon it was so cold that if Nelly wanted to untie a knot she had to pour boiling water over it first. 'Icebergs,' she wrote, and sailed carefully between them: some shaped like claws, others like archways, others like loaves of bread. One of them—low and flat like a paving stone—had a polar bear standing on it, and Nelly felt so sorry for him she considered inviting him on board. He looked

very thin, sad, and lonely, but he also looked hungry. He stood on the ice with his black claws touching the water, licking his lips and studying Nelly without blinking, and when he yawned she saw that his tongue and the inside of his mouth were black too, though his teeth were long and yellow. So she left him where he was and drew a picture of him in her log, small in the light of the wintery sun, which turned his fur pink and stretched his shadow out far behind him.

Pretty soon, the days grew so short that the sun no longer rose at all, and Nelly had to do her chores by moonlight. She chipped the ice off the decks, and then beat it from the sails, which glittered like steel. She plotted her course in her cabin by candlelight and practised juggling in the dark, which is the most difficult sort of juggling there is, and never broke a cup. And all the time it grew colder.

Nelly knew she was close to her destination when the wind started to bluster from every direction at once, and the ocean flowed in a circle. She had learned this from her

Explorer's Companion, and so she was not surprised when her compass also began to spin (as compasses do when they can no longer point north), or by the wonderful shifting colours in the sky, which are called the aurora borealis, or Northern Lights. She knew that there would be no land at the North Pole, only floating ice, and that if she fell into the water she would turn into an icicle in less than a minute. But funnily enough, just as Nelly arrived at the red cross on the postman's map, the icebergs seemed to get smaller, and there were fewer of them. Their sharp corners began to soften, and the water, very gently, began to steam.

When is a journey over? Between one breath and the next, the air, which had been so cold it was painful to breathe, thickened. A warm mist dampened Nelly's scarf, but did not thaw the icicles hanging from her rigging. Fog lay about the boat and glowed in the moonlight. It came up from the water and glittered as it froze. According to Nelly's calculations, she was now just a few miles from the North Pole, but instead of ice she found the ocean steamed like soup, and the fog was full of noises. Things slapped and gurgled, things snuffled and sighed, and in the background was a dull grumble like a distant freight train. One minute Nelly saw a shadow behind her that turned out to be her own shadow. The next she saw a shadow ahead that turned out not to be a shadow at all. It looked like a man standing with his arms stretched out in welcome, with long sleeves hanging down in tatters. He was thin and stiff and there was a light on top of his head and in either hand. And then she saw that the man was not a man, that his sleeves were sails, that his body was a mast, and that the mast was footed in the enormous hull of a broken-down ship. The tops of its sails were white and sparkling with frost, and the ragged bottoms flapped in the wind, and as Nelly sailed closer she could make out its name: *The Penny Black*.

Chapter
TEN

The Penny Black was not a warm or inviting ship. Nobody answered Nelly when she fired a flare, or whistled with her fingers in her mouth, or shouted through her ship's megaphone, unless you count the echo of her own voice, which was as strange to her in that place as if somebody else were speaking. There was nobody in the rigging or on deck, or at the wheel, or standing on the prow to welcome her. It was like talking to a ghost ship surrounded by white breath from another world, so that it was almost a relief that no flag was raised or boat lowered, and a definite mercy that the black dragon figurehead did not turn to stare at her.

Captain Peabody's ship stood dark and unmoving, as if to say, 'Come aboard if you dare, or if you have given up hope.'

So Nelly went aboard, because she had said she would find her father, and when she said a thing she meant it. She packed a duffel bag full of essentials, inflated the little rubber dinghy she had brought all the way from home, and rowed across, sending up puffs of steam with each dip of the oars. Then up the anchor chain she scrambled, hand over hand, past the snails that clung to the ship's sides like smooth warts, until she reached the top where nobody waited for her. The deck was grey and deserted, glittering with frost, and in the middle of it was an open trap door, like a hole in the top of the world.

It was not pleasant to be in a place like that, staring at a hole that looked like an open mouth or the entrance to a tomb, but Nelly went down anyway, although she did not like to imagine what she would find or how deep she would have to go. She went down because she had come so far already and did not want to go back home with nothing to show for her efforts. She felt for the stairs with her toes, and with her fingers for the rope banister, and it was like climbing into the empty shell of an enormous extinct turtle. But she kept her nerve, and when she came to the bottom she found a door with a strip of light shining around it.

'GENTLEMEN ONLY' said a sign on the door.

So Nelly went in.

It was quite a large room. Along one side was a glass-fronted bookcase. Along another were shelves with specimen jars that glittered in the light thrown from the fireplace and from green-shaded lamps set into the walls. There were a dozen or so battered leather armchairs around the fire—some green, some red—and behind one of them Nelly could see a small man in a sailor's uniform carrying a tray of drinks. Nelly was sure she had met him somewhere before and couldn't quite think where, but she knew the group of bearded men who sat in the armchairs immediately. They were the ones that stood behind Captain Peabody in the photograph in his study: the famous Gentlemen of the Exploratory Flotilla.

'Can't you read?' said one of them, lowering his newspaper and pointing to the door.

'I beg your pardon?' said Nelly.

'I said, can't you read?' repeated the man.

'No ladies,' said a second, rudely. 'That's all!'

'But I'm not a lady,' objected Nelly.

'Or girls,' said the first man, who wore

a monocle and had a silver whistle round his neck.

'What do you want, anyway?' asked a third, actually rising to his feet in indignation. His face was red, and his neck was thin, with a flap of skin that shook with rage. All of them were thin and they all seemed angry with her for not being a gentleman. Some were standing up shaking their fists; others glared over the tops of their newspapers, some with bushy sideburns, some with pointy beards—all clenching their pipes savagely between their teeth.

'I'm Captain Peabody's daughter,' shouted Nelly, stamping her foot, 'and a deputy of the Post Office! I've sailed a very long way on my own, through all sorts of dangerous situations. I'm tired and cold and hungry, and I want to see my father!'

'Well why didn't you say so in the first place?' said the Monocle.

'But Captain Peabody doesn't have a daughter!' objected a man with an enormous salt and pepper moustache.

And soon they were arguing amongst

themselves, huddled around the fireplace, in the sort of whisper that adults use when they don't want to be overheard, but that can actually be heard across a room. They wondered if they should give Nelly a glass of powdered milk or a biscuit, and where she should sleep, and when it came to the question of what bathroom she should use they almost came to blows. They argued about club rules, and somebody suggested Captain Peabody should be expelled, which provoked a particularly furious round of pipe clenching and newspaper waving until the man wearing the monocle called them to order.

'You say you're Peabody's daughter?' he demanded.

'I do.'

'And a deputy of the Post Office?'

'I am.'

'Then the easiest solution would be for you to speak to Captain Peabody yourself.'

'Here here!' shouted his colleagues. 'Quite right!'

'But where is he?' asked Nelly.

'Out,' said the Monocle, who was definitely the leader of the group.

'Up the mountain,' explained a gentleman with huge sideburns.

'The mountain?' said Nelly.

'That's what he said,' snapped the Monocle. 'Up the mountain with his rascally crew. The boatswain can take you to him.'

But the boatswain was nowhere to be seen, and when the Monocle blew his silver whistle nobody appeared.

'Little fellow in a sailor suit,' he said. 'Was here a moment ago.'

'My bag!' gasped Nelly, and found it had vanished too. She had put it by her feet and now it had disappeared, along with the boatswain, whatever a boatswain was.

'Confound the fellow!' said the Monocle. 'Pack of thieves, the lot of them!'

'But we must go after him!' cried Nelly.

'We?' said the Monocle, placing his hand on his chest. '*We*? Oh no, I hardly think so! He'll be halfway up the mountain already, and it's no place for ladies, or gentlemen for that matter: no place for any civilized person of any description whatsoever. Captain Peabody and his crew live up there like wild men; in fact they *are* wild. They've all gone native, to a man, and I'm afraid your father is by far the worst of them.'

'But you don't understand,' said Nelly, 'that bag had my turtle in it!'

'Too bad!' said the Monocle.

'Shame,' said another.

'Especially as turtle meat is so delicious,' added the man with the huge sideburns, with an expression on his face that suggested he'd eaten it before.

'But no use crying over spilt milk,' said the Monocle. 'Better stay here with us.'

'Even if we have run out of marmalade.'

'And rich tea biscuits.'

'And anchovy paste.'

'Even if we live like starving beggars on corned beef and tea,' said the Monocle. 'Far better to stay safely down here with us than to risk it up there. Even if you *are* a lady. Even if you have to use the officers'

bathroom. In fact, why not? You can use my towel.'

'But a moment ago you were saying I should go with that man in the sailor suit. You said it would be much the easiest thing. And now you're saying I should stay down here with you just because you don't dare go yourselves. And you call yourselves gentlemen! And explorers! Nonsense! You're just a pack of cowards!'

At which point there was a lot of shouting, followed by silence, and then some throat clearing as the Gentlemen of the Exploratory Flotilla twiddled the buttons on their waistcoats and tapped their pipes against the mantelpiece. They hummed and hawed, they went up and down on their toes, they stared at the carpet and the ceiling.

'You don't know what it's like up there,' said one.

'Giant snakes,' said another.

'Man-eating cats,' said a third.

'Red hot lava,' said a fourth.

'Red hot lava?' scoffed Nelly. 'At the North Pole?'

'Certainly,' said the man with huge sideburns. 'Don't you doubt it.'

'Well I don't care *what* there is,' said Nelly fiercely, 'if you don't take me, I shall go by myself.'

So off they went.

CHAPTER
ELEVEN

Nelly's guides put on fur hats and long scarves that hung very close to the ground. They wore tight-fitting jumpers and stout walking boots, and had canvas knapsacks packed with corned beef and thermoses of hot tea. Two or three of them carried guns, but the guns didn't seem to steady their nerves as they lowered a boat into the water, or as they rowed away from *The Penny Black* and Nelly's own ship. They kept glancing over their shoulders and shushing each other and straining their ears, and when the boat ran aground with a soft thump they all jumped at once.

'Eek!' said the man with the salt and pepper moustache.

'Shh!' said the Monocle.

'Land ho!' said Nelly, and so it was: land at the North Pole where there shouldn't be any land at all.

Out they hopped, one by one, and trotted across a beach of soft grey powder, and then onto a path where, here and there, wisps of steam curled up from beneath the rocks. But when Nelly asked her companions where the steam was coming from they hushed her very fiercely and told her that if she couldn't keep quiet they would all have to go back home.

'I mean it!' said the Monocle.

'This instant!' said the man with huge sideburns, holding his finger rigidly in front of his nose to show how serious he was.

So Nelly kept her questions to herself, although there were plenty of them: what a boatswain was; what a mountain was doing with steam coming out of it where there should only be floating ice; and if her father was still an explorer or had really turned wild. She wondered what had happened to him, and if he truly was so wicked now that he could turn Columbus into turtle soup.

'Impossible!' she whispered, and hurried after the men trotting ahead of her, although it was hard to keep up when her legs were so shaky and the ground beneath her feet felt like jelly. She had been at sea so long that dry land behaved exactly like water. It seemed to heave like waves, and Nelly often lost her balance, grabbing at anything that came to hand, which wasn't much.

Up they climbed, slithering on ice, then wading through snow that came over their knees, and at times Nelly wanted to shout at her guides to slow down, and at others to hurry up because she was so worried about Columbus. She thought of him in the duffel bag and wondered if he was frightened, then of his cake tin beneath her bed at home, filled with sand from the beach outside her bedroom window. She thought of him nosing for slugs in her mother's garden, or snoozing amongst the gooseberries, and she couldn't imagine really losing him. The idea made her mouth dry and her stomach queasy, so she concentrated on the ground in front of her, or the shapes of her guides ahead, growing dimmer as the fog grew colder and thicker. She thought of the quay at home where she had sat with her turtle beside her, plotting her adventure, and wished she had never come at all; because what was the point of finding her father if she lost her best friend? It was as though there was a ball of wool behind her ribs that was unravelling, and when all the wool was gone she would have nothing left at all.

Nelly climbed and the shapes of her guides grew fainter, so that at times she lost sight of them altogether. The fog closed around her, and she stumbled through it without really knowing if she was following or just wandering. All she knew was that she had to keep going because if she sat down she would fall asleep in the snow and never get up again. But if she did fall asleep maybe Columbus would talk to her., and then she wouldn't have to get up anyway because they would be together. So she sat down, and that was how the Monocle found her.

'Come on, come on!' he said. 'We're all

waiting for you.'

And he led her up the last bit of the mountain, to where the other gentlemen stood in a row, above the fog, with their backs to the starry night sky.

Nelly didn't know how long it had taken to climb the mountain, or how high it was, although it seemed very high indeed. Below her she could see the fog, rolling in a thick blanket, lit up by an enormous moon and the shifting colours of the aurora borealis. It was so beautiful that for a long time she stood looking at it, in silence, with the frozen polar wind blowing on her face.

And then she turned and found she was looking into another world.

On one side of the mountain it was winter, but on the other it seemed to be summer. Except it wasn't the other side of the mountain Nelly was looking at. She was standing at the summit looking down *inside* the mountain

from the rim of a crater so enormous she couldn't see over to the other side. Above her were the stars and the Northern Lights, and at her back the cold wind blowing around the pole. But down below the earth inside the crater was carpeted with millions of trees, green as broccoli, sending up a warm milky breath.

'It's like a dream,' said Nelly, biting her tongue to make sure it wasn't.

'A nightmare you mean,' corrected one of her companions.

'A living hell,' agreed the man with the huge sideburns, looking hopefully down the track which they had just climbed, as if he very much wanted to go back to the ship that minute and settle down in his armchair all safe and sound with a newspaper and a cup of tea.

'But I suppose we shall have to take you anyway,' sighed the Monocle, 'because, after all, you are only a girl.'

CHAPTER
TWELVE

Very carefully and slowly, as if he were talking to an idiot, the Monocle explained that Captain Peabody lived deep in the forest with his crew, and could be reached by a path that threaded between the trees. It was essential, he explained, that Nelly should not step off the path because the forest was stuffed with wild and dangerous animals.

'Spiders!' he hissed.

'Poisonous tree frogs!' offered one of the others.

'Yes, yes,' scoffed Nelly, 'and man-eating cats!'

She was very angry because the Monocle had called her a girl—or *only* a girl—and was about to ask him to whom he thought he was talking. But her companions said that if she uttered another word they would leave her where she was.

'Hush!' they said, and '*Shhhhh!*' and their faces went purple with the effort of not making too much noise. They told her not to touch anything and *certainly* not to put anything in her mouth; to keep her eyes peeled for things that might fall from above, and her ears pricked for things that might jump out from either side. If they met Captain Peabody's crew, they said, she should keep perfectly still and not look them directly in the eyes, because that would definitely upset them, and as for Captain Peabody himself, they begged her not to provoke him, even if she was his daughter.

'They worship him as a god, you know,' said the Monocle, and just as Nelly was about to tell him not to be so silly, up from the trees, very softly, came the sound of drums.

Down the path they went, and as the trees closed over their heads Nelly forgave her guides a little for being so rude because she could see how frightened they were, and how uncomfortable. Up by the rim of the hollow mountain it was still quite cool. White-haired monkeys looked down at them through rustling leaves, and the ground was crunchy with frost. But the further down they went the warmer the forest became, the thicker the leaves, and the darker the space beneath them. There were squeaks in the undergrowth, and scratchy chirrups. There were coughs and barks, sometimes quite close and sometimes far away, and once a line of chickens shot out suddenly from behind a bush. But when Nelly asked what chickens were doing at the North Pole she was shushed so passionately by her comrades that she gave up asking, and began to feel, in any case, that there might be some reason to be careful.

As the party climbed down deeper into the volcano, the forest became thicker and wilder, with long cruel thorns and huge flowers that might have been red

or yellow or blue, but in the dark had no colour at all. There were plants shaped like clasped hands and others like hairy heads, and things that looked like plants but turned out to be animals: a crested bird that looked like a fern, an enormous spider Nelly had mistaken for a bunch of bananas. It became so hot that the gentlemen removed their jumpers, then their flannel shirts, until they were walking in their vests. But Nelly (slashing at the undergrowth with her red-handled cutlass) kept on her dungarees because they protected her from the thorns and things that rustled along the ground. Tiny lights shone out from the darkness, but they were not stars, because the stars were hidden by the forest roof, although now and then the moon sliced through a gap in the leaves, making everything look as though it had been drawn with chalk on a blackboard.

And all the time the drums sounded louder, so that it was hard to tell what was inside and what was outside. She began to imagine

that everything around her was breathing and humming, gasping and thudding, as though the blood rushing in her ears was also in the trees and leaves and the enormous fluted bowls of tropical plants where rain water had gathered. Things brushed her face or tickled her armpit, or hastily got out of her way, making a loud commotion in the undergrowth. Nelly was always flinching, always stopping a scream, until, walking through a pool of moonlight, she looked down and saw a giant centipede, all spiny and glistening, crawling across her boot, and she really did scream.

She screamed, and the moment the scream was out of her mouth, something right next to her roared so loudly that it took the scream away, and her companions, the so-called Gentlemen of the Exploratory Flotilla, ran off into the jungle without a backward glance, leaving Nelly all alone.

Being alone in a jungle is not at all like being alone at sea, because the sea does not care whether you are alone or not. It blows a ferocious storm and you think it is trying to drown you, when in fact it does not know you are there. But the jungle does know. It likes you to be alone. It *wants* you to be alone. Because when you are alone it is easier for the jungle to get at you.

In the jungle you feel you are being watched, and you probably are. You are alone amongst a crowd of things that want to eat you, or sting you, or bite you with poisoned fangs. At any moment you might be pounced on or skewered, and there is absolutely nothing you can do about it except to listen very carefully and keep your eyes peeled, which is what Nelly did. She listened to the so-called Gentlemen of the Exploratory Flotilla crashing about, getting further and further away, and occasionally she heard gunshots and shrieks. Very possibly, she thought, her companions were being eaten alive, just as she was probably going to be eaten alive.

I should never have come, she thought. I should have stayed at home with Columbus and looked after my mother.

But she was not eaten, and when something did step out onto the path it was not a lion or tiger as big as a horse, but an ordinary house cat. It was black with a small tuft of white at its throat, and its eyes, when it turned to look at her, were golden.

'Here I am,' the look seemed to say, though the cat spoke no words. And then

it winked slowly and walked off down the path with its tail in the air.

So Nelly followed the cat, just as she had followed the explorers, through thorns and knuckly roots, and leaves like soft leather gloves, because what else was she going to do? She had no idea where she was, and no idea where she was going. So she trusted the cat, however difficult it was to pick it out in the gloom. Sometimes she could see the whole of it, and sometimes only its tail floating above the undergrowth like a question mark; and all the while the drums were getting louder and the air more stifling, until, pushing through what looked like two giant lettuce leaves, she stood on the edge of a clearing so hot she felt like she'd opened an oven door.

CHAPTER
THIRTEEN

Standing in the shadow of the giant lettuce, Nelly took it all in: the giant trunks of trees, the tables spread with white tablecloths, and, dancing round a pool of fire, just as she had seen them in Columbus's dream at the very beginning of her voyage, a group of small men, naked except for the things her mother had knitted. Amongst them, Nelly noticed, was the boatswain—no longer in his sailor suit as he had been aboard *The Penny Black*, but dressed just like all the rest (despite the heat) in woolly hat, scarf and mittens. They all danced round in a circle; their eyes glittering, their beards bristling, their bodies tattooed with fish, birds, and animals that seemed to have a life of their own in the light of the fire, which cast the dancers' shadows right across the clearing and onto the trunks of the trees.

It was all exactly as Columbus had shown it, all those months ago as Nelly lay fast asleep in her cabin: the white mountain steaming like a kettle, the forest, the fiery lake which was actually a pool of lava. Columbus had seen it all, and now here was Nelly's old friend, too, lying on a rock by the lava, fast asleep as usual, with his beaky nose scratching the painted surface of the stone.

Only one thing was missing: Captain Peabody himself. But then, out of the forest on the other side of the clearing stepped a tall man dressed in grubby linen pyjamas and a three-cornered hat, walking quickly with a stick as if he were late for an appointment.

Later Nelly would say that it is one thing to be abandoned by your father as a baby and quite another to be forced to watch as his crew prepare to roast and eat your turtle. But there was nothing she could do.

It was as though she were made of hollow clay and couldn't move or say a word, or even close her eyes, but had to stand on the edge of a dream, cutlass in hand. She watched Captain Peabody step out of the forest, and his men part before him. She watched him walk up to the pool of lava and raise his stick, and, as the drumming stopped, stand for a moment in the silence. She watched Columbus lying asleep on his stone, and noticed that his shell was painted too—with flowers and stars, a sun and a moon.

And then Captain Peabody lowered his stick and something happened that Nelly had not expected. The sun rose. It came up from behind the trees and its light shone down into the clearing, striking Columbus's shell and spreading out across the ground, licking across green moss and falling on her father's crew, who lifted up their faces and their arms and began to sing. Sunlight spread across the clearing as if spring itself were a song, eclipsing the glow of the lava, and finally reaching the place where Nelly stood, alone in the shadows. And then Columbus lifted up his beaky head and yawned, and it was as though she were released from a spell. She walked out from beneath the trees, through the singing men, who turned and smiled at her as she passed, and as she took her turtle in her arms, Captain Peabody opened his and widened his eyes in delight and amazement.

'Nelly!' he said. 'What are you doing here?'

'Collecting a parcel,' said Nelly.

'Of course you are,' said Peabody. 'And just in time for the party.'

CHAPTER
FOURTEEN

Nelly had never been to a party before, not a real one. Christmas lunch aboard *The Penny Red* didn't count because the postman-pirate's crew were not the party sort. They did not do back somersaults, or juggle burning branches, or breath fire, or stand on each other's shoulders, one on top of the other, in a human pyramid twenty men high and walk around with the top man stealing the captain's hat and pretending to give orders. They did not imitate the sounds that birds make so beautifully that it was impossible to tell the difference, or growl like tigers or whoop like baboons, or weave the jungle into a dancing song that made Nelly feel as though the whole forest and everything in it were living inside her.

But Captain Peabody's crew did. When the sun rose they sighed and rustled like

wind in the leaves. They sang a song about springtime and said goodbye to winter, and burned all their clothes in the lava pit—their woolly scarves and hats and mittens—then dived, shouting, into a lake which Nelly hadn't seen before, because in the dark it's harder to see water than it is to see fire. They splashed about and the boatswain ducked them under, one after another, including Captain Bones Peabody, who waded in still wearing his pyjamas. But when it came to Nelly's turn the boatswain didn't duck her straight away. Instead he smiled and put her hands on his head so she could duck him first. Then he pushed her under. And when she came up again he gave her Columbus, who had been swimming around in search of something tasty.

After the singing and dancing were over, and the feast, which had been entirely vegetarian, was eaten, the crew put leaves over their faces and slept in the sun. Around the clearing the tablecloths were all stained with juice and the plates were empty. Butterflies moved amongst the first flowers and the trees were full of birdsong as bright and sweet as the sunlight filtering down through the leaves. Nelly sat with Columbus cradled in her arms and everything was so peaceful that she was tempted just to listen to the bees buzzing and the gentle snoring of the crew, who seemed to understand exactly how to live in a forest inside a hollow mountain at the top of the world. Part of the secret, apparently, was never to say a word unless you were singing. But Nelly found her head was full of unsaid things and she couldn't rest until she'd said them.

'So have you been here all this time?' she began, a little crossly.

'Oh no!' said Peabody, who was sitting beside her with his chin on his knees and his beard hanging down his shins. And he explained that he had intended to be back in a year but things had not gone according to plan. One gale had blown him this way, another that. He had been kidnapped by bandits, chased by pirates, and only escaped dying of thirst by inventing a tea bag that could suck the salt out of seawater.

'It makes a perfect cup every time,' he explained modestly, 'and tastes delicious with a slice of lemon, which as you know is an excellent fruit for preventing scurvy.'

'You might have sent me some of those bags,' said Nelly, thinking how thirsty she had been before she met the postman-pirate.

'But I did,' said Peabody. 'Don't tell me you didn't get them?'

'No, I didn't,' said Nelly.

'What about the cufflinks?'

'What cufflinks?'

'Or the bone kangaroos, or the performing mice, or the fossilized sea anemones?'

'Not a single one!'

Captain Peabody looked so put out that Nelly felt almost sorry for him, and said he had sent her birthday and Christmas presents every year since the beginning of his voyage, starting with a dozen painted snails and a turtle egg in a cake tin.

'So that one at least got through,' said Nelly, tracing the freshly painted flowers on Columbus's shell with her finger.

'Yes,' said Peabody, 'that one at least got through.'

Later Nelly would say that her father was fond of explanations, which was lucky because he had a great deal to explain. At the North Pole, he told her, the night lasted all winter, and the day all summer, so that there was only one night and one day a year. Nelly had arrived just in time for the spring equinox, which explained all the excitement, and the party, as well as the business with Columbus, who in the crew's eyes was a magic turtle.

'We found him,' explained Peabody, 'on a Pacific island, along with the snails. The snails lived in the trees, but Columbus and his brothers and sisters were down on the beach, still in their eggs, buried in the sand. When the eggs began to hatch, the baby turtles ran down to the sea, but I'm afraid very few of them made it into the water because they were eaten by hungry seagulls. It was such a horrible sight that the crew became instant vegetarians, and when they found an egg unhatched they brought it to me and begged me to save it.'

'And here he is.'

'Yes, and here he is, which explains all the fuss. You see the crew made up a story about him. They said that, although he had gone away, one day he would come back to them, and when he did everything would be born again. Which in a way it has been.'

Captain Peabody smiled.

'They call him The Turtle That Dreams The World.'

'And do they worship me, too?' asked Nelly.

'I'm not sure they know who you are.' said Captain Peabody. 'I'm not sure anybody does; not yet.'

Which made Nelly feel a little sad, so that for a moment they sat together listening to the birdsong pouring down from the trees.

'Where did it all come from?' she asked.

'You mean the mountain?'

'Yes.'

'And the forest?'

'Yes.'

'And everything in it?' whispered Peabody. 'Yes, impossible.'

CHAPTER FIFTEEN

So Nelly heard her father's story from the beginning: how he had set out with his crew and fellow explorers on a voyage of scientific discovery; the countries he had visited; the rivers he had sailed up; the many strange plants and animals he had collected. When Captain Peabody spoke his eyes lit up and his hands moved in the air. Sometimes he would growl like a bear, or gape like a fish. Sometimes he would stop and gasp, as if he were actually seeing a particular wild pig or petal-nosed mole for the first time, and Nelly thought she saw them too, so that when he told her how, just as he thought his voyage was coming to an end, he had been trapped in drifting pack ice close to the North Pole, she could hear the planks of the ship begin to splinter.

'It was a huge sheet of ice,' said Peabody,

'stretching out on every side, and every day it closed in tighter, making a sound like an ogre grinding his teeth. We were being crushed by the ice, and at the same time we were so hungry that I'm ashamed to say my colleagues, the so-called Gentlemen of the Exploratory Flotilla, considered eating our cargo. But the crew wouldn't let them. The boatswain posted a guard on the door to the hold and hid the key to the larder. For three whole months we lived on porridge oats and melted snow.'

'And then?'

'A gigantic underwater explosion,' whispered Peabody. 'An eruption from the seabed that broke through the ice so close to the ship it set our sails on fire. One moment the sky had been cold and blue, the next it was full of lava and chunks of rock hurtling all over the place, big as grand pianos. On and on it went, and every moment we expected to be sent to the bottom. And then it was over and there was a mountain sticking out of the sea wrapped in fog so thick you'd never know it was there unless

you'd seen it being born.'

'A volcano?' said Nelly.

'A volcano,' confirmed Captain Peabody, 'at the North Pole. A miracle so unexpected that if we had sat down for a month dreaming up ways we could be saved—a tribe of wandering Inuit, a hot air balloon, a friendly whale—we would never have hit upon it. A volcano in the coldest place on earth!'

'Amazing!' breathed Nelly.

'Staggering!' agreed Peabody.

'Incredible!'

'Yes! But do you want to know the most extraordinary bit? No sooner could we hear ourselves speak than my courageous gentlemen colleagues, men who called themselves explorers, were whining about going home.'

'Home?'

'Yes, home,' growled Peabody, frowning so hard that he was glaring at his own eyebrows. 'Men who claimed to be scientists! Adventurers! Blubbering about hot baths and buttered toast with a brand new volcano standing right in front of them, unexamined, unnamed, without so much as a flag planted on it. But my crew and I were more curious. We launched a boat and went ashore. We climbed to the summit. We peeked over the rim, and inside we found earth as rich and good as chocolate pudding.'

'But not actually chocolate pudding?'

Peabody laughed.

'No, but would it surprise you to know that this entire forest came from a jam jar?'

'Nonsense!'

'But it did. Our ship was full of specimens from all over the world—every imaginable plant and animal, every rare and beautiful thing, and other things that at first glance you might think ordinary. We started by planting a lettuce seed, then some radishes, and, after that, soft fruits: blackcurrants, raspberries. Up here at the North Pole one day lasts all summer, and the volcano's crater protects it from the Arctic wind. Perfect for tomatoes! In fact, everything grows so fast that very soon we had solved the food problem entirely, so we began to bring the animals up for walks, first the small ones, and then the bigger fellows too. Only the Gentlemen of the Exploratory Flotilla stayed below, because they are cowards and have no appetite for anything but black pudding and feather beds.'

'Are they really so bad?'

'The worst! Which is why I've left them to rot. These days, they live down there with the snails, and we live up here in the forest. Only the boatswain bothers to go down to see what they're up to, and only because he has a soft heart.'

'But, all the same, if it hadn't been for them I wouldn't be sitting here with you now,' said Nelly.

And she told her father how she had met the Gentlemen of the Exploratory Flotilla aboard *The Penny Black*, and how they had agreed to take her up the mountain, and about the roar, and the black cat that had led her to the clearing.

'You see?' laughed Peabody. 'At the first

sign of danger, off they run.'

'But, all the same, they did their best,' said Nelly, and she thought about how the Monocle had come back to fetch her when she had given up and sat down in the snow, and how without him she would certainly have frozen to death. And then she wondered if he and his friends really had been eaten by lions and tigers, or if they were only lost and needed finding.

'What's a boatswain?' she asked.

'He's the chief of the ordinary sailors and looks after the ship,' said Peabody. 'The ropes, the carpentry, the larder, that sort of thing. It comes from an old word meaning "boat servant", and ours takes his duties very seriously.'

'And what about you?'

'What about me?'

'Do you take *your* duties seriously? Shouldn't you look after your own ship?'

'And live down there with those nitwits? Am I an explorer or a paperweight?'

'I don't know, but I always thought that's what a captain did. That he stayed with his ship, whatever the weather, even if it was sinking.'

Nelly fiddled with a thread that had come loose from her cardigan.

'Don't you *want* to come home?'

And for the first time Peabody looked as though he were at a loss for words. But then he cleared his throat and blew his nose on his handkerchief, which was blue with white spots.

'Want?' he said, 'Of course I want! But don't you see? Look, Nelly, this mountain is made of volcanic rock that erupted from the middle of the earth, and inside it there's a place for every creature and plant that lives on it, as well as several others that live nowhere else but right here, in this crater. Take the moss you're sitting on. It's not really moss at all. It's a very close relation to a kind of seaweed that lives on the seabed miles underneath the North Pole. How does it survive out of the water? In this heat? Nobody knows! Or why there are daisies in

it. There are bananas in this forest and three-toed sloths from Panama, as well as hedgehogs, scarab beetles, badgers, cougars, slow-worms, and a species of salamander that can live in boiling water. Some of these things can be found outside the mountain, and others not. Some like the cold and others the heat, some wet some dry, and there's a place for them all. All of them are at home here, and so are you, too, if you'd only see it as I do.'

'So you really have gone native,' said Nelly.

'Whatever that means,' said Peabody, staring up at the trees.

'I don't know. Something about forgetting where you

come from, I suppose.'

'Native means "to be born in",' said Peabody, taking a small rainbow-coloured butterfly on his finger. 'And it's true, I wasn't born here. But there again, where was I born? And what does it matter? I'm an orphan, just like my crew.'

'Well I'm not,' said Nelly, except she didn't say it she only thought it, and felt suddenly very close to crying, except she did not want to cry, so instead she asked her father what name he'd given to the mountain.

'Penelope,' replied Peabody, 'after your mother.'

'A lovely name,' said Nelly, wiping her eyes. 'And now I think it's time to send out a search party.'

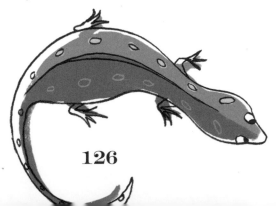

Chapter
SIXTEEN

They found the Gentlemen of the Exploratory Flotilla up a boab tree, very tired, very angry, and very frightened. The Monocle was hardly recognizable, until he put his eyeglass back in, and the man with the ginger sideburns had one trouser leg missing. They sat up in the branches like ramshackle crows with all their feathers bent, or middle-aged explorers who have scrambled up into a place from which they cannot scramble down, and so must sit for as long as it takes for somebody to come and rescue them.

And this was exactly what had happened. There were no lions or leopards or ravenous tigers pacing around the base of the tree, or any reason at all why they should not have come down if they had wanted. But they were too frightened, which made

them angrier still, so that as soon as they saw Nelly, Captain Peabody, and the crew (who had done the tracking), they all began to shout at once: about how uncomfortable and hungry they were, and the wild animals that had hunted them through the forest—bears, snakes, giant rats—and were just getting to the bit about man-eating cats when they were interrupted by a roar even louder than the one that had scared them away in the first place.

'That's it!' shrieked one.

'That's him!' screamed another.

'Mummy!' wailed a third.

'Courage!' shouted Nelly, drawing her cutlass.

But Captain Peabody just laughed and pointed to his feet where the black cat that had led Nelly to the clearing rubbed its head against his ankle.

'Here's your culprit,' he said.

'Nonsense!' said the Monocle. 'That's just an ordinary pussycat.'

'But his mother was a panther,' replied

129

Peabody. 'Big roars, small paws.' And leaning down he scratched the cat behind its ear until it purred like a kettle coming slowly to the boil. 'His name is Marco Polo and he sleeps at the foot of my bed.'

'Well I'm glad you're such good friends,' said the Monocle, but he didn't sound as though he meant it, and after clearing his throat he made a speech.

'You laugh at us and call us cowards,' said the Monocle, 'but it wasn't you who led Nelly up the mountain, and I'll bet it wasn't your idea to come and rescue us, either. You are aware, I think, of a gentlemen's agreement, which you have broken in so many ways that I don't like to list them all in front of a lady. You promised us we would be back in a year, and you broke your promise. You smuggled away our cargo, which was theft, plain and simple: *stealing*.'

The Monocle said the word very clearly

and slowly to show how serious stealing was.

'And then you deserted your ship and swaggered about up here in your pyjamas and three-cornered hat, forgetting your friends and your family, and everything we had promised each other before we set out.'

'But you could have come with me!' said Peabody.

'And lived up here like earwigs in a hollow tree stump?'

'Or sailed home; nobody's stopping you.'

'You know very well we don't know how. But what's the use of talking? You're a disgrace to the Flotilla, Peabody. You don't look after people. Your crew worship you, but you're not a god, and you're not a captain, either. You've lost your way completely, and you don't see it because there's nobody up here to tell you who you are.'

'Who I am?' said Nelly's father in a deadly voice, 'Who are you to tell me who I am?'

'I am a person who made a promise and kept it,' said the Monocle, 'whereas you are a person who made a promise and broke it. But if you won't listen to me listen to your daughter.'

And suddenly everybody was looking at Nelly: the Gentlemen of the Exploratory Flotilla from the boab tree, Captain Peabody's crew with their heads tilted, and Captain Peabody himself, not laughing any more, but pale and serious.

They all stood waiting for what Nelly had to say, but at first she couldn't say anything. She thought about Columbus and how she'd felt when she thought she'd lost him, and her mother at home, knitting. She thought about the rhubarb patch, and the snails clinging to the taps in the bathroom, and her father's study, empty for so many years. She thought of her own little boat, which had sat rotting for so long at the end of the pier, and her voyage and all the hardships she had suffered. She thought of her promise to find her father, and how she had kept it, and how at the end of her quest nothing was turning out as expected.

'Oh, I don't know,' she said, 'you talk a lot about yourselves and go on about savages and cowards and gods and captains, but nobody's interested in what *I've* done or who *I* am, and the fact is I've done a lot. I have a ship and *I do* know how to sail it, and tie knots, and plot a course, and weather a storm. Columbus and I found our way to the North Pole all by ourselves and have had so many adventures with pirates and waterspouts and so forth that I could spend all day talking about them, which in the North Pole is a long time. But you don't want to ask me about it. You behave exactly as you did before I arrived, and it makes me feel as though I might as well leave you to it.'

At which point there was a dreadful silence, except for the leaves rustling in the trees.

'Oh Nelly,' whispered Peabody, and

getting down on his knees he begged her to forgive him. 'I am so sorry.'

CHAPTER
SEVENTEEN

The Gentlemen of the Exploratory Flotilla were so tired from their ordeal that as soon as they got back to the clearing they went to sleep in hammocks strung between the trees. And Nelly slept too, so deeply that when she woke she had no idea where she was, or what had happened. Columbus was at her feet, and for a moment she thought she was at home in her mother's house, or aboard her own ship, or aboard *The Penny Red*, except there was no postman sitting beside her holding a jug of water with a slice of lemon in it.

And then she remembered she was in her father's cabin, on the top bunk, which explained why her nose was so close to the ceiling. She was lying on a thin mattress stuffed with something not-so-soft—possibly horse hair—and from below came the sound of a kettle boiling and the delicious smell of toast and coffee.

'Jam?' said Captain Peabody. 'Quince or rhubarb?'

'Rhubarb,' said Nelly, noticing that the sound of the kettle was Marco Polo purring in a rocking chair, winking up at her with golden eyes.

'And now,' said Peabody when they had finished eating, 'I think it's time for you to tell me all about your adventures.'

So Nelly told him about her ship and how she had made it ready, the knitting of the sails, and Columbus's dream of the mountain and the crew and of the cabin they now sat in. She told him about the storms and the whales and her encounter with the postman, and her father gasped and applauded and told her she was a worthy descendant of her ancestors, who were all, on account of Peabody being an orphan, on her mother's side: an admiral; a great aunt who wore a wig and smoked a cigar and commanded a ship of her own; and a whole string of pirates, explorers and scientists in every corner of the world.

'And does the postman really hate you?' asked Nelly.

'It would certainly explain why none of my letters get through,' said Peabody, grinding his teeth, and he explained how they had grown up together in a naval orphanage, and how at first they had done everything together. They had even shared a stamp collection and agreed to name their first ships after their favourites—a penny black and a penny red. But then they'd won scholarships to the Officers' Academy, and at the graduation ball they had fallen in love with the same woman.

'My mother?'

'Your mother. She was wearing a green dress and she cried when she saw my buttonhole—a rose—because she had never seen one before. You see, her father (your grandfather) was a captain; not of a ship, but of a submarine, and so she grew up underwater in a sort of furnished tin can, without much at all by way of flowers or scenery, or company in general. Which explains, I think, how quiet she is, as well as her passion for knitting, gardening, and cards.'

'And what about the postman?'

'Your mother gave me the first dance and promised him the second, but he never got it. He said his life was ruined in the time it took to finish a waltz.'

'Which reminds me,' said Nelly, rummaging in her duffel bag, 'he asked me to give you this watch.'

'Ha!' said Peabody. 'You see? Five minutes fast.'

'And what about his crew? Are they orphans like yours?'

'Yes, they are. We all are. Except that the postman and I became officers, whereas they did not.'

'Life is unfair,' said Nelly.

'Yes it is,' agreed Peabody. And for a while they sat together in silence, smelling the blossom that flowered along the branches of the trees like a million hearts breaking, watching the sunlight pick out the crumbs on their plates and make the jam in the jam jars glow pink and red.

Nelly's father lived in a tree house with a stove for cooking and a bucket on a string to lower things down or pull them up. There were square windows in the wooden walls, and shelves lined with cactuses, specimen jars, model boats, and Captain Peabody's illustrations of plants and animals. He and Nelly sat on rocking chairs drawn so close together that they could both reach the coffee jug on the stove single-handedly, and as they sipped they discussed navigation and seamanship, the art of war, diplomacy, botany, and household management. When one conversation ended another sprang up instantly to take its place, and when they had finished with the things that came off the top of their heads, Captain Peabody showed Nelly his diary, which was identical to hers—crowded with writing and sketches and columns of numbers.

'I left my other one at home,' he said, 'in the drawer of my desk.'

'I know,' said Nelly, and pulled it out of her duffel bag.

So they sat together comparing notes and exchanging stories, and everything was

as peaceful as it could possibly be until Peabody asked Nelly how long she was staying.

'Not long,' she said. 'In fact, it's time I got back. Because, you see, I promised Mother I would be home in a year, and when I make a promise, I keep it. Which reminds me of something.'

'What's that?'

'That today is my birthday.'

'Your birthday!' gasped Peabody, turning white and sucking air through his teeth as if somebody had stamped on his toe. 'But yes, I admit it. I forgot!'

'Actually it was yesterday, if you can talk about yesterday when a day lasts all summer. But all the same.'

'What can I give you?' asked Peabody, 'Just name it. Anything at all!' And she could tell from his face that he meant it.

'Then I'd like you to come home with me,' said Nelly.

'Of course,' said Peabody, looking relieved. 'I thought it was already decided. Just give me a little time to pack.'

CHAPTER EIGHTEEN

Peabody's crew would not allow their captain to leave without a party, or without singing Nelly the ballad of her adventures, which they called 'The Dreams of Columbus'. They played on drums and tin whistles and violins, and sang in voices that sometimes sounded

like the wind blowing and sometimes like waves crashing, and sometimes like the roaring of an erupting volcano. They sang about the readying of her ship and the battle with the pirate and the roar in the jungle, and it was all so real that for Nelly it was like having the whole adventure again, without the boring bits.

Nelly listened as they sang about the coming of 'The Turtle that Dreams the World' and 'The Secret Knitter', which was the title they had given her, because of the night-time knitting of her ship's woollen sails. They sang about her courage, and the loneliness of being orphans, and the beauty of the forest so skilfully that Nelly hardly noticed where her own story ended and theirs began.

And then they served a birthday cake and sang happy birthday and the boatswain presented Nelly with the key to the larder, which is the highest honour a boatswain can bestow.

'Won't you need it yourself?' she wondered.

But the boatswain said no. He and his men

were happy where they were, and would not be accompanying her back across the water because they had no families of their own. They would miss her, and they would miss their captain, but they wanted to continue living amongst the trees—eating salad in summer and baked potatoes in winter. They would come as far as the beach to collect their mail, and then they would say goodbye.

'But who will sail *The Penny Black?*' wondered Nelly.

'We'll have to make do with the Gentlemen of the Exploratory Flotilla,' said Captain Peabody. 'Though heaven knows all they are good for is reading newspapers and eating sandwiches.'

So off they went, up the path, through giant fig trees, then peach trees and banana trees, and finally through apple and plum trees— gorgeous with white-haired monkeys, splendid in the polar sun—out onto the rim of the volcano with the wide blue sky above them, where Captain Peabody, who was still wearing his pyjamas, grumbled about the cold.

But the crew were not cold, because they carried Peabody's specimens, packed into enormous canvas trunks, and neither were the Gentlemen of the Exploratory Flotilla who whistled as they walked along with their hats and gloves. In fact, of the whole party they were the happiest. They were so happy it was almost as if they were home already, and all the way down the icy side of the mountain they talked about hot baths and soft beds and delivering lectures about their adventures to important universities. They awarded themselves professorships and medals, and as they stepped out onto the beach the Monocle was halfway through accepting a prize for discovering not only the most northerly volcano in the world, but inside it the most abundant variety of life, when Captain Peabody froze and held up his hand.

'Quiet,' he hissed.

'What's the matter?' asked Nelly.

But Peabody only pointed his finger out to the bay.

It wasn't Nelly's own boat that stood nose to nose with *The Penny Black* in the fog, but a ship so exactly its twin it was as if each were staring at its own reflection: both carrying many sails; both with the same narrow-jawed figurehead at its prow. There were no two ships in the world so like one another, and in the fog it was impossible to tell which was black and which was red. Then out of the gloom sang a voice.

'Am I late?'

And onto the snout of the dragonish figurehead stepped a man Nelly recognized, though she could not see his face nor the colour of his breeches.

'The rogue!' breathed Peabody.

'The postman,' whispered Nelly.

'The pirate!' squealed the Gentlemen of the Exploratory Flotilla.

'Ahoy, Peabody, is that you?' called out the postman-pirate. 'You have something I want. Can you guess what it is?'

When Nelly came to draw a diagram of the battle that followed in her diary (or log), it looked a little like this: aboard *The Penny Red*, which flew the Jolly Roger above a red silk handkerchief, the postman-pirate stood on the very tip of his dragon's nose

Icebergs

shouting 'Invincible!' though nobody could hear his voice above the sound of his guns.

Aboard *The Penny Black*, meanwhile, which flew a plain black flag, Captain Peabody, his teeth bared in a terrible grin, returned fire, blowing out the cobwebs from the barrels of his cannons, shaking off the rust, and making such a roar that the mountain itself seemed to mutter and stir in its sleep.

One moment the two ships stood apart, lost in the fog and their own smoke; the next they charged together like fire-breathing dragons biting each other and tangling their wings.

'Insatiable!' screamed the pirate, somer-saulting from his high place like a circus tumbler, and Captain Peabody leapt down to meet him, clutching the cutlass that his daughter had lent him—the one with the red handle.

As for Nelly, she stood with Columbus on the deck of her own small ship, ready to light the curly tails of her Chinese dogs, but she couldn't tell which of the larger ships to fire on, or – as the grappling irons flew and the boarding parties swarmed across the gunwales – which crew belonged to

which captain, or which captain to which crew. All she heard was the din of the battle and occasionally, rising above it, Peabody trying to guess what it was the pirate wanted.

'Is it my ship?'
'*Guess again!*'

SWASH!!

'Is it my stamp collection?'
'*Guess again!*'
'Is it the Admiral's Cup for Night-Time Navigation?'

Up and down the two men fought, and sometimes Nelly, peering through her telescope, could make out her father's three-cornered hat, and sometimes a glint of gold from the postman-pirate's brightly buckled red boots. But then around they'd spin and she couldn't tell who was who.

'Don't play games!' shouted Peabody, clambering into the rigging.

'Don't play games?' laughed the pirate, clambering after him. 'But I love games! Look, here's one: first to the top is king of the castle.'

And up they went, now swiping at each other with their cutlasses, now gripping their blades between their teeth as they crawled toward the square platform, high above the water, that sailors call the fighting top.

'Fire below!' shouted Peabody, making the final dash.

'Cheat!' shrieked the pirate, cutting at his ankles. But down below fire really had broken out, and as it swept across the decks of both ships, the crew—brightly coloured or suited in grey—plunged into the steaming water and struck out toward the shore.

'Jump!' shouted Nelly. 'Or you'll be burned alive!'

But neither Peabody nor the pirate heard her. To and fro they fought, round and round the mast or teetering out along the spars like tightrope walkers. Sometimes they jabbed at each other through the rigging; sometimes they embraced each other like the brothers they almost were. And all the time the fire grew hotter and higher, rolling out across the decks, shrivelling the ropes, licking at the shredded ends of the sails, setting off a case of flares that went up like sizzling fireworks: red, green, and blue.

'Oh Columbus,' said Nelly, 'they'll be roasted!'

But Columbus only looked at her and gaped. The noise was upsetting him and the bright light hurt his eyes, and when something exploded with a boom louder than any cannon he pulled his head into his shell and lay there like a stone.

'Gunpowder!' shouted Nelly 'Watch out for the powder!' And sure enough the powder kegs standing by the cannons were exploding one by one, or sometimes three at a time, sending up sprays of splintered wood and mangled metal.

'Boom!' they went. 'Boom-boom-boom!'

There were not two ships, now. *The Penny Red* and *The Penny Black* were one huge bonfire, with flames reaching greedily down to the powder magazines on the lower decks, and toasting the soles of the boots of the men who fought at the very tip of the highest mast, pirouetting around the crow's nest.

'Is it an animal?'

'*Guess again!*'

'Is it a vegetable?'

'*Guess again!*'

'Is it a mineral?'

'*Guess again!*'

'Is it my naturally red hair?'

'*GUESS AGAIN!*'

'Then I give up! What is it?'

'A *waltz, Captain, a waltz—five minutes of your time!*' screamed the pirate as three things happened at once.

First, with a fantastic, acrobatic leap and a twist, the pirate captain sent Peabody's cutlass whirling end-over-end into the furnace. Second, Nelly, in a desperate effort to drown the fire before it reached the magazines, lit the fuses of her Chinese dogs and aimed below the waterline.

'Perhaps we can sink them,' she whispered, 'and put it out that way.'

But the sound of her dogs barking was swallowed by an explosion so huge that it flattened the water like a giant hand.

KA-BOOM! said the mountain, by way of the third thing. And Nelly's mind went dark as she joined Columbus in his shell.

155

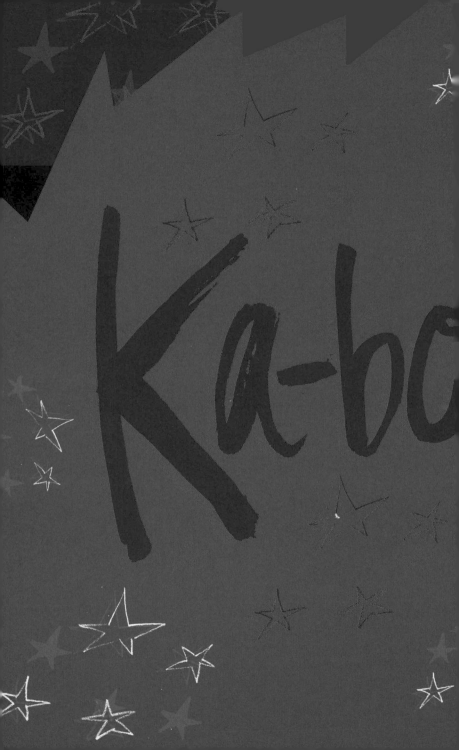

CHAPTER TWENTY

The Battle of Penelope Bay, or Penny Bay, or Nelly Bay, as it became known depending on who was telling the story, ended with an eruption, as if the volcano were reminding everybody how it had been born and how things might end. But on this occasion it was only a reminder—a tremor, a belch, a warning—leaving a new front door in its side, with a river of red hot lava running out of it, greying as it cooled. The mountain gave one more shudder, and then it was still, while down in the bay the Gentlemen of the Exploratory Flotilla (who had spent the battle standing on the beach, biting the ends of their fingers, and covering their eyes) paddled to and fro with the crew, looking for survivors.

They found Nelly on the deck of her ship and brought her round with a shot of emergency rum, which the Monocle produced from a silver hip flask.

'Good girl,' he said as she sipped and choked, 'brave girl,' and wiped away a tear because he was so relieved she was alive.

He told her she had more courage and good sense than the whole lot of them put together, and henceforth he considered her an honorary gentleman with a lifetime subscription to the officers' mess and an armchair just like his own.

But the Monocle no longer had a chair, or a ship, or, it seemed, a captain, because *The Penny Black* and *The Penny Red* lay at the bottom of the bay; blown to bits by their own powder, sunk by the bronze dogs, or shattered by the volcanic blast, it was hard to say. They searched for a long time through the wreckage—bits of canvas and splintered planks (some with snails still clinging to them), blackened ropes, the charred snout of a dragon—but of Peabody and the pirate captain they found no trace. They looked for hours, quartering the bay, hunting round and round in circles, and had almost given up hope when they discovered them a little way off, muffled by the fog, using the crow's nest as a life raft, arguing heatedly as they took it in turns to paddle with their remaining cutlass.

'Ah Nelly!' said Peabody.

'Just in time,' said the postman.

'We were having a bit of a dispute.'

'A scientific matter.'

'If you were standing on your head at the top of the world,' said Peabody, 'would your feet still be pointing north?'

'Or south?' ventured the postman.

'I thought you were dead,' said Nelly in a shaky voice.

'Dead?' said Peabody.

'Dead?' echoed the postman, but, of course, when they told him what had happened he couldn't remember a thing about it.

'Not that I deny it,' he added apologetically, 'and it's a pity about the ships.'

'We'll just have to build some new ones,' said Peabody cheerfully, and the thought of it put a light in his eye, so that by the time they had got back to shore he had already organized both crews into work details: some to chop wood for the planks, some to smelt the brass, others to collect oil and resin for the varnish.

'Bravo!' said Nelly, and agreed to stay on for as long as it took to knit the sails.

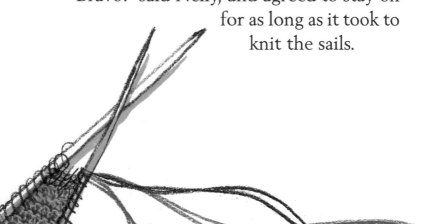

CHAPTER
TWENTY-ONE

So Nelly knitted a set of sails, red and black, and while she was at it the new ships grew up from the beach: first the runways, then the scaffolds, then the heavy keels, which stop a ship tipping over in rough weather. There was no shortage of wood in the forest for planks, or metal in the rocks for nails, or hands to do the work. Bit by bit they came together, two identical vessels, side-by-side, rising up from the soft ash under the volcano.

But long before even the ribs of the hulls were finished Nelly was done and ready to go, and nobody could persuade her to stay a minute longer, because, she explained, she had promised to be back in a year, and when she made a promise she kept it. And in any case, she had missed the apple blossom and if she didn't hurry she would

miss the rhubarb, too.

So she handed out the mail, which included fresh winter clothing for the crew, as well as pyjamas for Captain Peabody, and anchovy paste and rich tea biscuits for the Gentlemen of the Exploratory Flotilla. And then she made her goodbyes.

'Goodbye,' said the Monocle, and presented her with his silver whistle.

'Goodbye,' said the postman, and reminded her again about the red handkerchiefs.

'Goodbye,' said Captain Peabody, and gave Nelly a letter to deliver, as well as a beautiful polar rose and a jam jar with holes drilled in the lid.

'The rose,' he said, 'is for your mother, and so is the letter. But the jam jar is for you and is named after you: *Lycaena Nellia*, to give its proper Latin title. Don't open it until you get back home.'

And then he told her that he loved her and was proud of her, and that he would follow her as soon as his new ship was seaworthy.

'Goodbye,' said Nelly, although she didn't actually say it, because she couldn't find her voice, so she thought it instead.

So off she went, leaving her father a kiss as a keepsake, with Columbus by her side and her hold full of good things, and also the fog, the cold and the snow that covered the mountain. She took the frigid sunlight of the polar summer and the secret forest Peabody had shown her, and his promise that he wouldn't be far behind.

Nelly sailed through the ice of the Arctic, along the shadow of the hungry polar bear, on into the warmth where dolphins raced beside her. Near the equator she looked for *The Penny Red*, only to remember that it was at the bottom of the sea along with its sister, *The Penny Black*. She dodged a waterspout and a whirlpool, talked to whales, and ran so low on things to eat that when the last storm hit she was too weak to fight it. So she reefed her sails, fixed her wheel with a knotted handkerchief, and went below, where she lay in her hammock with her head beneath the blankets.

Nelly didn't know how long the storm lasted, because she slept all through it like a dead person, and when she woke up found she had come back home again—to the apple tree and the rhubarb, and the little house with red roof tiles and green curtains. The tide was out and the *Nelly* was sitting on the mud at the end of the pier—or jetty, or quay, or pontoon, or whatever you want to call it—with the water lapping around her keel. There was not a speck of paint left on her hull. Her masts were cracked and grey. Her wheel was spotted with woodworm, and of the knitted sails, which Nelly had patched so carefully on her journey, there was not a trace.

But if Nelly was worried she had only dreamed her adventures (and she had always loathed stories that ended that way), there were certain unmistakable signs to the contrary. Around her neck hung a silver whistle and an iron key. Beneath her pillow was an envelope with her mother's name on it in looping green ink. Beside her hammock, standing in a glass of water, was a polar rose

as crisp and fresh as new snow, and when Nelly unscrewed the lid of *Lycaena Nellia*, out flew a butterfly with wings the colour of rainbows.

'But where's Columbus?' she wondered, wriggling her toes. And for a moment there was a horrible cold lump in her stomach as she wondered if she might have left him behind, or if he'd been washed overboard in the storm, until going up on deck (with her butterfly on her shoulder) she noticed a nail had worked itself loose from the planks, and that snagged around it was a woollen thread.

So she drew it in, hand over hand, loop upon loop, until over the gunwales came her turtle, heavy as a medium-sized cannonball, with his toenails varnished, his shell painted with flowers, and a look in his eye that she knew very well—as if he'd been somewhere very interesting, but wasn't going to say where it was.

ABOUT THE AUTHOR

Roland Chambers has had some adventures of his own. He's been a pig farmer, a film maker, a journalist, a pastry chef, a cartoonist, a teacher, a private detective and an author. He's also lived in a few different countries, including Scotland, Australia, Poland, America and Russia. Now he lives with a professor next to a cake shop in London. He owns two cats, two children and two guinea pigs.

WATCH OUT FOR ANOTHER NELLY ADVENTURE, COMING SOON!

Ready for more great stories?
Try one of these ...

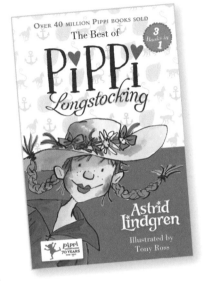

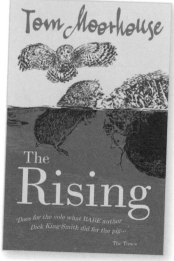

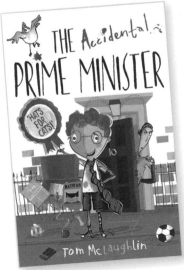